Keepin

by Mich

Contents

Protecting the House   2

The Delivery Truck   10

Lions and Tigers and Bears   14

Literacy Footprints, Inc.

Chapter 1
Protecting the House

Bella has an important job.

It is Bella's job to protect the house.

Every day after breakfast,

Bella gets up on the couch

and looks out the window.

She watches for intruders.

Bella does not like animals coming into her yard.

She does not like the chipmunks.

She does not like the squirrels.

She does not like any chipmunks or squirrels in her yard.

Chipmunks and squirrels are intruders.

4

The chipmunks love walking
right in front of the window.
Whenever Bella sees them,
she starts to bark and scratch
at the door to go out.

One day, Bella called to Rosie.
"It's a chipmunk. Come on, let's get it!"

Bella and Rosie ran out the door
after the chipmunk.
The chipmunk ran across the yard
and up a tree.

"Woof, woof!" barked Bella.

"Woof, woof!" barked Rosie.

"We never catch the chipmunks,"
said Rosie.

"Why do we try? They are too fast!"

"We will catch one someday," Bella said.

Bella and Rosie went back to the house. Bella got back up on the couch and began to look out the window again.

After all, it is Bella's job to watch for intruders.

Chapter 2
The Delivery Truck

Bella's ears pricked up.

She heard something coming.

Rumble, rumble, rumble.

A truck was coming down the driveway!

Usually no one would let Bella out of

the house if a car or truck was coming,

but today the door was open.

Bella ran out, and Rosie ran out, too.

"It's the delivery man,"

Bella called to Rosie.

"I don't like him — let's get him!"

The truck stopped. A man got out and carried a box to the house. Bella ran to check out the truck. "Grrr," she said sniffing the truck. "Grrr!"

Then she ran to look at the box. "What is this?" she said suspiciously.

Bella turned to look at the truck, but it was gone.

"I will get him next time," she said.

Chapter 3
Lions and Tigers and Bears

Bella looked out the window,

watching for intruders.

Bella's ears pricked up.

She could hear the rustling of leaves.

"Is something in the woods?"

she wondered.

"Come on, Rosie," she called.

"Let's go!"

The two dogs ran out the door barking.

Bella and Rosie ran across the yard to the edge of the woods.

"There's an animal in the woods," said Bella.

"Is it a squirrel?" asked Rosie.

"No," said Bella.

"What is it?" asked Rosie.

"Maybe it's a lion," whispered Bella.

"Oh, no," said Rosie.

Rosie began to shiver.

"I'm afraid of lions. It might eat us!"

"Maybe it's a tiger," whispered Bella.

"Oh, no," said Rosie.

She shivered even harder.

"A tiger might eat us!"

17

Bella thought for a moment.

"Or maybe it's a bear.

There are bears in the woods."

"A bear!" said Rosie. "A bear!

A bear might eat us!"

"I will protect you Rosie," said Bella.

"We are not lions, or tigers, or bears,"
called some little voices.
"We are the five little dogs.
Come into the woods and play with us!"

Bella and Rosie ran into the woods to play with the five little dogs.

"I'm so glad you aren't lions, or tigers, or bears," said Rosie.